ROTARY
INTERNATIONAL

This book is dedicated to all friends of nature—
young, old, human, or kappa.

Published by Tuttle Publishing, an imprint of Periplus Editions (HK) Ltd., with editorial offices at 364 Innovation Drive, North Clarendon, Vermont 05759 U.S.A., and at 61 Tai Seng Avenue #02-12, Singapore 534167.

Library of Congress Cataloging-in-Publication Data

Seki, Sunny, 1947-
The last kappa of old Japan : a magical journey of two friends / told and illustrated by Sunny Seki. -- 1st ed.
p. cm.
Summary: In 1860s Japan, young Norihei saves the life of a kappa, one of the mythological beings who keep the water clean, and the two become friends, but changes brought by the Industrial Revolution force the kappa to leave, only to return when Norihei needs him most. Includes historical and cultural notes.
ISBN 978-4-8053-1088-5 (hardcover)
[1. Folklore--Japan. 2. Kappa (Japanese water goblin)--Fiction. 3. Friendship--Fiction. 4. Environmental protection--Fiction. 5. Japan--History--1868---Fiction.] I. Title.
PZ8.1.S4545Las 2010
398.2--dc22
[E]

2009032890

ISBN 978-4-8053-1088-5

Distributed by

North America, Latin America & Europe
Tuttle Publishing
364 Innovation Drive
North Clarendon, VT
05759-9436 U.S.A.
Tel: 1 (802) 773-8930;
Fax: 1 (802) 773-6993
info@tuttlepublishing.com
www.tuttlepublishing.com

Japan
Tuttle Publishing
Yaekari Building, 3rd Floor
5-4-12 Osaki
Shinagawa-ku
Tokyo 141 0032
Tel: (81) 3 5437-0171;
Fax: (81) 3 5437-0755
tuttle-sales@gol.com

Asia Pacific
Berkeley Books Pte. Ltd.
61 Tai Seng Avenue #02-12
Singapore 534167
Tel: (65) 6280-1330;
Fax: (65) 6280-6290
inquiries@periplus.com.sg
www.periplus.com

First edition
14 13 12 11 10 10 9 8 7 6 5 4 3 2 1

Printed in Hong Kong

The Last Kappa of Old Japan

A MAGICAL JOURNEY OF TWO FRIENDS

TUTTLE PUBLISHING
Tokyo • Rutland, Vermont • Singapore

Our story begins in Old Japan, just before the time of electricity. In the peaceful countryside, full of nature and fresh running streams, there lived a boy named Norihei. His family had been farmers for many generations.

Norihei grew up around healthy country food, with village people who shared their fresh produce. But he did not just eat; he had to cook and clean up too! Most importantly, he learned to serve each dish correctly, because in Old Japan it was the custom for children to serve older people.

Norihei knew that farming requires soil, sunshine, and water. He was proud that his cucumbers were growing especially big this year.

One day while working in his garden, Norihei heard a loud moan. Astonished, he saw a strange creature with webbed hands and spots on his back. Norihei had never seen one, but he was sure … this must be a kappa!

"Are you okay?" Norihei asked the kappa.

The creature replied in a weak voice, "I've been out of the water too long because I've been eating your tasty cucumbers. Now I'm too weak to go home!"

"Wow! Kappas really do exist!" thought Norihei.

Norihei splashed water on the kappa, who quickly regained his strength.

"Oh, thank you. You're not mean like other people. I will be forever grateful to you for saving my life!"

Norihei had heard that kappas were scary, but he liked this one. So he gave him some cucumbers to take home.

One day while Norihei was fishing, the kappa appeared again.

"I was wondering ... what's your name?" he asked.

"I'm Norihei," he replied.

The kappa smiled and said, "My name is Kyu. Follow me, and I will show you where to catch the biggest fish!"

Kyu taught Norihei a new way to swim, and Norihei showed Kyu how to sumo wrestle. They quickly became good friends and gave each other nicknames – "Kyu-chan" and "Nori-bo."

“Nori-bo! Be careful! That eel will give you a shock if you touch it!” Norihei was fascinated as Kyu-chan showed him the secret wonders of the water world.

The two friends often met to play in deep watery canyons. But not far away, a railroad was being built. Japan was changing rapidly.

One afternoon two railroad workers saw Kyu-chan and Norihei skipping stones. They whispered slyly, “We should catch that kappa! We can sell it to the aquarium … or maybe the circus!”

Norihei saw them coming. “Kyu-chan, run! They’re trying to catch you!”

“Don’t worry, Nori-bo! When I reach water, I can use magic to escape!”

“Hurry! There is a well is right over there!” said Norihei.

Kyu-chan was upset. “Why are they trying to catch me? I didn’t do anything wrong!”

Just in time, Kyu-chan jumped head first into the well. SPLASH! The men peered inside, but all they saw were ripples.

"We missed him! He got away!"

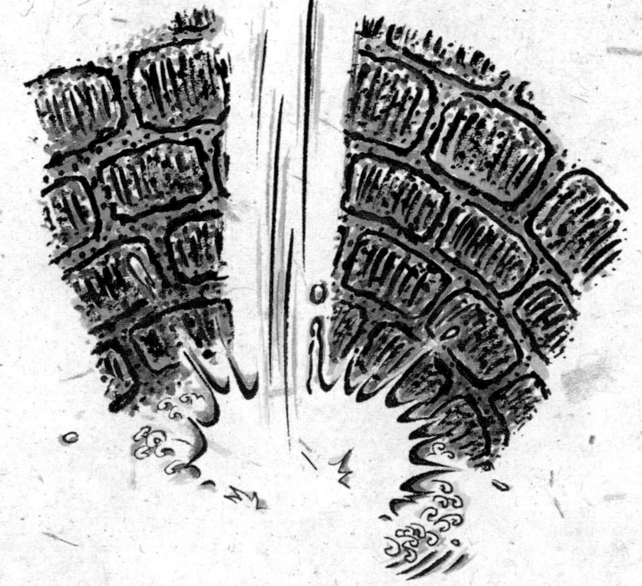

A few days later Kyu-chan told Norihei some sad news.

“Nori-bo, my family says we have to move. Our job is to keep the water clean, but this area is getting dangerous. My parents are worried. But before I go I want to give you this crystal necklace. It’s shaped like a water drop. If you ever need help with water, drop this into a stream and call me.”

After that day, Norihei would not see his friend for a very long time.

Twenty years passed, and the once peaceful countryside was now a busy town with electricity and big factories.

Norihei was no longer a boy, but a grown man. He had a wife named Hana, a baby girl named Kaya, and a dog named Maru. Norihei still lived in the same house. But the front part was now a restaurant.

Norihei's restaurant was very busy. He was a good chef, and people liked his fresh new recipes. And Hana was a hard-working manager.

One day, while Norihei and Hana were very busy, baby Kaya ran outside to chase a butterfly. Only Maru the dog saw what happened.

Suddenly Maru barked, “Arff-arff!”

Norihei and Hana ran outside. Kaya’s pinwheel was on the ground, but she was gone. It seemed that she had fallen into the stream.

小唄教授いたし〼
龍
おもちゃ
駄菓子
あたり屋

In a state of panic Norihei and Hana ran, frantically asking anyone if they had seen a baby.

Hours passed, evening came, and the search crew found nothing.

"We're very sorry," they apologized, "but we can't work in the dark. We'll have to wait until morning."

Norihei just gazed at the water. He had never felt so sad in all his life. Then suddenly he remembered the necklace he had received from his old friend.

"This is my last hope. Kyu-chan … please … if you are still out there, find our baby!"

Norihei took a deep breath and dropped the necklace into the water. Hana looked puzzled. He told her about the kappa and the promise of the necklace, but her face was still full of doubt and despair.

It was after midnight, but Norihei and Hana couldn't sleep. The only sounds they heard were the ticking of the clock and the howling of the wind. They were beginning to lose hope.

Suddenly, Maru leaped up and barked. Someone was knocking at the door. Norihei and Hana looked at each other.

"Who could it be?"

"Kyu-chan! ... Is that really you?" Norihei shouted.

It was the kappa. He was much older, and he was carrying a baby.

"My baby!" cried Hana. They were overjoyed.

"Sorry for the delay," Kyu-chan said as he stumbled in. "I had to come at night so I wouldn't be seen. I searched everywhere to find your daughter, and I kept my promise!"

"Thank you!" said Norihei.

The two friends hugged, crying tears of joy.

"How have you been, Nori-bo?"

"I'm fine, Kyu-chan. But you have some cuts and bruises! Let me clean them for you."

Norihei said, "When you first came in, I thought I was seeing your father!"

"Yes, I do look a lot older ... That happens to kappas when the environment is not right. Actually, the rest of my family have all died, and I'm the last kappa alive." Norihei remembered that the kappa's job is to keep the water clean.

"If you die, who will take care of the water?"

Kyu-chan looked serious. "It will have to be you humans."